Have you heard about Epic! yet?

We're the largest digital library for kids, used by millions in homes and schools around the world. We love stories so much that we're now creating our own!

With the help of some of the best writers and illustrators in the world, we create the wildest adventures we can think of. Like a mermaid and narwhal who solve mysteries. Or a pet made out of slime.

We hope you have as much fun reading our books as we had making them!

epic! originals

SCAREDY MONSTER

MEiKA HASHiMOTO
illustrated by STEVE LAMBE

Andrews McMeel
PUBLISHING®

Part One

SCAREDY MONSTER

Loses a Tooth

Meet Scaredy Monster.
He has big teeth.
He has sharp claws.
He has an enormous
ROAR!

Scaredy Monster is sorry.
He hopes he did not
frighten you.

In fact, Scaredy Monster
has a secret.
Do you want to hear it?

All right.
Come close.
Scaredy Monster will whisper
his secret to you.

Scaredy Monster is NOT
a scary monster.
He is a SCARED monster.

Why is Scaredy Monster scared?
He opens his mouth to show you.
Do you see it?

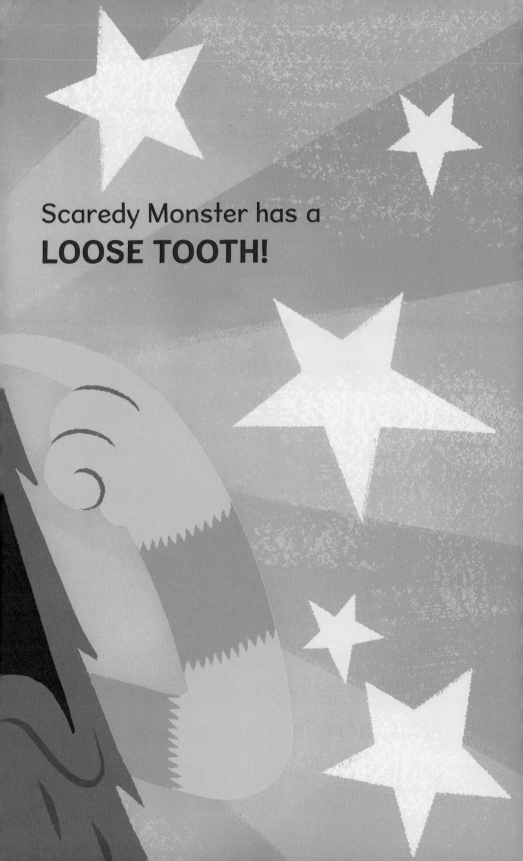

Scaredy Monster has a
LOOSE TOOTH!

He is worried because he has heard terrible stories about monsters who lost their teeth.

One monster swallowed her tooth in her sleep. Now there is a forest of teeth inside her tummy.

Another monster lost a tooth,
AND IT NEVER GREW BACK.

Scaredy Monster does not know
if those stories are true.

But he still does not want to lose
his tooth. He makes a plan.
He finds EXTRA STICKY
peanut butter in the cupboard.

Scaredy Monster smears
the peanut butter all over
the top of his tooth.
There!
It is stuck.
There is no way his tooth
can come loose!

But then, Scaredy Monster
realizes something.

Peanut butter tastes good.

REALLY good.

Uh oh. There is no more peanut butter to keep his tooth stuck in his mouth.

Scaredy Monster must find a new plan.

He tries marshmallows.

They do not work.

He tries gum.

Gum is sticky.
But it is also MESSY.

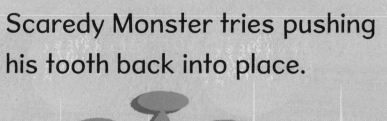

Scaredy Monster tries pushing
his tooth back into place.

He hurt his hand because his tooth is TOO POINTY!

The next morning at breakfast,
Scaredy Monster mashes his food.
He is scared to chew.
Mommy Monster asks him
what is wrong.

Scaredy Monster opens his
mouth. He shows Mommy
Monster his loose tooth.
He begins to cry.

Mommy Monster hugs
Scaredy Monster.
She tells him not to worry.
Losing a tooth is normal.

A new one will grow back.
And it will be BIGGER
and SHARPER than ever!

31

Scaredy Monster wipes
the tears off of his fur.
He will be brave. He will try
not to be scared anymore.

Scaredy Monster eats breakfast.
He bites down.

SCAREDY MONSTER'S TOOTH POPS OUT!

Losing a tooth was not scary.
It was easy!

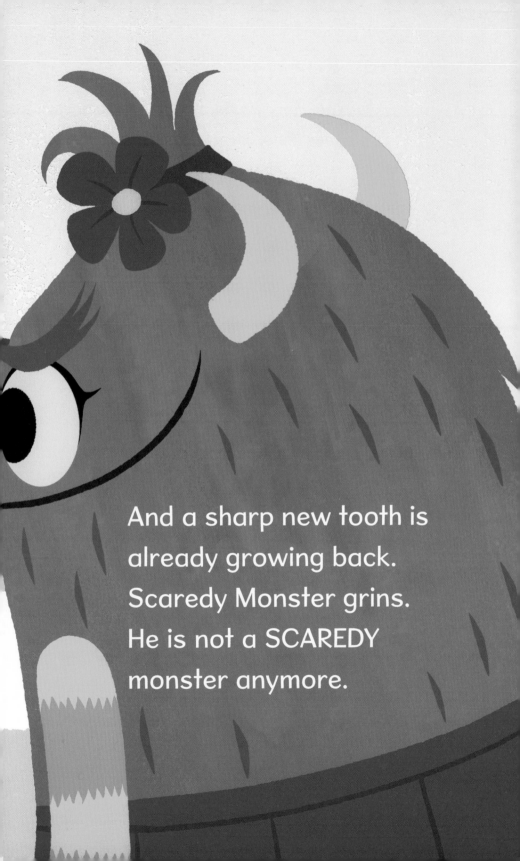

And a sharp new tooth is already growing back. Scaredy Monster grins. He is not a SCAREDY monster anymore.

Part Two
SCAREDY MONSTER
Rides a Bike

One sunny afternoon,
Scaredy Monster goes out to play.
He gets on his tricycle.

His tricycle is old.
It is too small.
It **CREAKS** and **MOANS**.

Scaredy Monster pedals
down the block.

CREAK. MOAN. CREAK. MOAN.

Scaredy Monster sees a yard sale.

40

His eyes
grow wide.

His heart
beats fast.

CREEEEAK!

Scaredy Monster stops his tricycle.

Scaredy Monster walks
over to a bike.

It is red. It is shiny.
It is just the right size.
It is PERFECT.

Scaredy Monster has a plan.

He hurries home.

He goes to his bedroom.

He dumps out his piggy bank.

Clink, clink, clink!

Scaredy Monster runs back
to the yard sale.

He buys the shiny, red bike.
He wheels it home.

That night,
Scaredy Monster
has a dream.

He dreams
he is the
FASTEST,
BRAVEST,
BEST
biking monster
in the world!

The next morning,
Scaredy Monster
cannot wait to ride
his new bike.
Mommy Monster
asks if he wants
bike lessons.

Scaredy Monster says no.
He can learn to ride
all by himself!

Scaredy Monster puts on
his helmet.
He hops onto his bike.

Scaredy Monster
starts to move—TOO FAST!
He tries to put his feet down—
TOO HIGH!
He cannot touch the ground!
Scaredy Monster does not know
how to stop!

Scaredy Monster wobbles.

He tips.

He FALLS!

Scaredy Monster is hurt.
Scaredy Monster is scared.
Scaredy Monster does NOT
want to ride his bike anymore!

Mommy Monster helps
Scaredy Monster get up.
They head home.

Mommy Monster cleans and
bandages Scaredy Monster's cut.
She wipes his tears.

Mommy Monster hugs
Scaredy Monster.
She tells him that trying new things,
like riding a bike, can be scary.
But with a little practice,
riding a bike can be really FUN.

Mommy Monster and
Scaredy Monster go back outside.
Mommy Monster picks up
the shiny, red bike.
She lowers the seat.

Scaredy Monster gets on his bike.
Now he can touch the ground!

Mommy Monster shows
Scaredy Monster how to push off.

She shows him how to balance
and how to steer.

The bike wobbles.
Scaredy Monster puts
his feet down to stop.

He is safe!

Scaredy Monster tries again.

And again.

And again.

Balance! Steer!

Mommy Monster helps. **Push off!**

Now comes the next part.
Mommy Monster shows
Scaredy Monster how to PEDAL.

Scaredy Monster takes a
deep breath.

He pushes off. He balances.
He steers. He pedals.

Mommy Monster lets go
of the seat,

and...

...SCAREDY MONSTER
IS RIDING A BIKE!

Scaredy Monster is glad
he kept practicing.
Mommy Monster was right.
Scaredy Monster LOVES
riding his bike.

WHEEEEEE!

Part Three
SCAREDY
MONSTER
and the Slumber Party

Scaredy Monster is excited.
His first slumber party is tonight!

Mommy Monster gives
Scaredy Monster
an overnight bag to pack.

Scaredy Monster packs

pajamas,

clean clothes,

a toothbrush,
and
toothpaste.

He finds a sleeping bag
and a pillow.

Finally, he puts
Teddy Monster in the bag.
Scaredy Monster has
never, EVER spent a night
without Teddy Monster.

Mommy Monster and
Scaredy Monster
go to the car.

Oh, no!
Teddy Monster falls
out of the bag.
Scaredy Monster
does not notice.

SAY BOO

Mommy Monster drives
Scaredy Monster to
Timmy Monster's house.
Scaredy Monster gets out of the car.
Mommy Monster kisses him goodbye.

Scaredy Monster goes
into the living room.

He sees other monsters
building a pillow fort.

Scaredy Monster helps out.
He puts the last pillow
on a GIGANTIC fort!

Next, Scaredy Monster plays
Pin the Tail on the Dragon.

Scaredy Monster wins!

At dinnertime,
Scaredy Monster chomps
on a big slice of pizza.
He LOVES his first slumber party!

At bedtime, Scaredy Monster
puts on his pajamas.

He brushes his teeth.

All of the monsters get
into their sleeping bags.
Timmy puts on a movie.
Timmy's mommy turns off the light.

In the dark,
the monsters watch the movie.
The movie is spooky.
TOO spooky.

Scaredy Monster starts
to get scared.

Scaredy Monster looks
for Teddy Monster.
Teddy Monster is gone!

Now Scaredy Monster
is REALLY scared.

One by one, the monsters fall asleep.
But not Scaredy Monster.
Scaredy Monster is WIDE AWAKE.

Outside,
the wind howls and moans.
There are shadows.

And maybe even
A HORRIBLE
MONSTER.

Scaredy Monster pulls
the sleeping bag over his head.
He misses his bed.
He misses Teddy Monster.
He misses Mommy Monster.

Scaredy Monster sits up.

He begins to cry.

Timmy's mommy hurries

to the living room.

She asks Scaredy Monster

what is wrong.

Scaredy Monster says
he wants to go home.
Timmy's mommy is nice to
Scaredy Monster.
But she is not Mommy Monster.

Timmy's mommy
calls Mommy Monster.
Mommy Monster says
she will come right away.

Mommy Monster arrives.
She tells Scaredy Monster
it is okay to feel scared.

Everyone gets scared sometimes.
Mommy Monster tells
Scaredy Monster he was
brave to ask for help.
She has something to help Scaredy
Monster feel better.

It is TEDDY MONSTER!

Scaredy Monster hugs Teddy.

He feels better.

He feels braver.

Scaredy Monster tells
Mommy Monster
he wants to stay.
He goes back inside.

Scaredy Monster
gets into his sleeping bag.
He holds Teddy Monster
close.

Timmy's mommy
turns off the light.

Good night, Scaredy Monster.
Happy slumber party.

About the Author

Meika Hashimoto grew up on a shiitake mushroom farm in Maine. After graduating from Swarthmore College, she worked in the mountains before taking a job as a children's book editor in New York. She loves to hike, rock climb, bake cinnamon buns, and wear warm slippers.

About the Illustrator

Steve Lambe is an illustrator of picture books and a character designer for animated television. His book credits include *Teenage Mutant Ninja Turtles*, *Blaze and the Monster Machines*, *Fanboy & Chum Chum*, and *Strange Scout Tales*. For TV, Steve has worked on *The Powerpuff Girls*, *Teen Titans Go!*, *Hilda*, and *The Fairly OddParents*, earning one Daytime Emmy Award, an Annie nomination, and a Reuben nomination.

Andrews McMeel Publishing
a division of Andrews McMeel Universal
1130 Walnut Street, Kansas City, Missouri 64106

www.andrewsmcmeel.com

Epic! Creations, Inc.
702 Marshall Street, Suite 280,
Redwood City, California 94063

www.getepic.com

20 21 22 23 24 SDB 10 9 8 7 6 5 4 3 2 1

ISBN: 978-1-5248-5522-2

Library of Congress Control Number: 2019950720

Design by Wendy Gable

Made by:
King Yip (Dongguan) Printing & Packaging Factory Ltd.
Address and location of manufacturer:
Daning Administrative District, Humen Town
Dongguan Guangdong, China 523930
1st Printing – 12/30/19

ATTENTION: SCHOOLS AND BUSINESSES
Andrews McMeel books are available at quantity discounts with bulk purchase for educational, business, or sales promotional use. For information, please e-mail the Andrews McMeel Publishing Special Sales Department:
specialsales@amuniversal.com.